Dream
Big!

Pool of Secrets

Volume 3

Written by: Nicole Brook

Illustrated by: Mike Anthony

The Amazing Adventures of Abigail Andrews

Pool of Secrets

Volume 3

Nicole Brook

LoveLight Creations

LoveLight Creations

The Amazing Adventures of Abigail Andrews – Pool of Secrets
@2015 by Nicole Brook. All rights reserved.
Published by LoveLight Creations
PO Box 5155 Drayton Valley, AB T7A 1R4
lovelightcreations.com

First published as an e-book through LoveLight Creations in paperback
LoveLight Creations. This is the second edition of this novel.
Cover design and Illustrator: Michael Anthony
2021. All rights reserved.
Editor: Eileen Harrigan

Library and Archives Canada Cataloguing in Publication

……………………………………………………..

…………………………………

………………………………………………………….

…………………………………………..

To Megan Dixon, an inspiring girl with an amazing imagination who fit perfectly into this book.

Thank you for sharing your talent and dreams with me. Keep writing and always show your superpower to the world.

Table of Contents

Chapter One
Splash

"Make sure you fill it up to the top!" Abby shouted as her mother turned on the hose to fill her little plastic pool. Abby loved that pool. Since the first day of summer, she had been waiting to swim in it, but it had rained non-stop! This was the first time she could use it. When she saw the sun shining brightly that morning, she ran outside and carefully pulled it out of the garden shed before her parents were awake.

Her parents surprised her with the pool for her ninth birthday. The sides were adorned with waves of different blue colours and mermaids with sparkly silver fins and flowing hair. She was enchanted with it the moment it caught her eye in the toy store. She called it Mermaid Tides because she imagined that she was actually swimming with the mystical creatures when she splashed in the pool. Abby loved swimming so much that it was the only time she enjoyed changing out of her favourite blue overalls and green T-shirt.

"Are you ready for your swim?" asked Abby's mother. Abby stood, waiting in her bright red swimsuit that had large, yellow flowers on it. Just as she was going to answer her mother, she realized she was missing something very important.

"I can't forget that!" she said to herself before she dashed into the house and up the stairs to her room.

Crash! Bang! She frantically searched through her toy box, throwing all sorts of toys onto the floor, but she still couldn't find it. She began to feel defeated, but then she spotted something underneath one of her teddy bears.

"Could it be?" she asked herself as she reached the very bottom of her toy box. "Yes, I found it!" Her smile was so big she was sure an alien could see her teeth from Mars!

She returned outside with a replica of a white cruise ship with the words Abigail's Voyager painted in red on its side. It was the same red as Abby's swimsuit! The ship was a gift her grandfather made for her with instructions to go on many special adventures with it. Having a big imagination was one thing that she and her grandfather shared.

"I'm all ready to go. Are you done filling up the pool?" Abby asked, all set to jump in.

"Yes. I'll just be in the flower beds if you need me, have fun!" Abby's mother grabbed her gardening gloves and headed towards the beds.

"Yippee!" Abby shouted as she quickly climbed over the edge of the pool and splashed down into the cool, refreshing water. She tipped her head back just enough that the ends of her blond pigtails broke through the water's surface. She stayed still for only a few seconds, just to cool off, then popped upright and started to play.

"All aboard!" Abby said as she docked her ship in front of her. "Mmm . . .," she hummed, trying to mimic the sound of the ship's engine. She looked down as she pushed the boat in circles around her and watched as the movement created mini waves that gently splashed against her stomach. Abby pushed the boat faster and faster when she felt a warm breeze rustle through her pigtails and she heard magical chimes swirl around her.★

Abby looked up and smiled when she saw that she was no longer in her pool or her backyard. She felt a wooden floor underneath her feet, she saw blue skies above her head, and she heard a soft humming noise that was all too familiar. She was overjoyed when she discovered where her imagination had taken her.

Chapter Two

All Aboard

Abby was on a small cruise ship, just like the one her grandfather made. She eagerly ran to the ship's wooden railing and looked over the edge to get a glimpse of the side. There it was, in bold red lettering, the words Abigail's Voyager. Abby lifted her head and smiled, instantly getting lost in her surroundings. The ship was slicing through deep, luscious blue waters that seemed endless. She took a deep breath in, and the scent of fresh salt tickled her nose.

As the ship was much bigger than her toy, she couldn't wait to explore it, and it didn't take her long to learn what the ship had to offer. Swimming pools where kids splashed around as their parents rested on nearby blue and white chairs. A playground on the far end of the ship, complete with a bright yellow swing set with green seats and a sandy brown slide.

Abby made her way around the playground and stood at the back of the ship, or the stern, which is what her grandfather taught her. She watched as the ship created graceful waves that moved through the water, much like her boat back home, only this time the waves were much bigger.

She continued to explore the ship and saw that one side of the deck was lined with cement sidewalks, grass, spruce trees, and even a few shops; she almost forgot that she was on a ship! She rushed over and peeked through one of the shop windows. Her blue eyes lit up when she saw ice cream containers lined up row-after-row.

Abby smacked her lips as she studied the different kinds of frozen treats: some with nuts, some with candy, and some with her all-time favourite—mouth-watering chocolate chips! She leaned her face close against the shop's window, wanting to see more when she heard a voice from behind her.

"If you push any harder, you might go through the window," a little girl said with a giggle. Abby giggled too as she turned towards the girl. She was the same height as Abby, with short, light-brown hair that just passed her chin. She was wearing a pink bathing suit and white shorts. "I haven't seen you around here before; what's your name?"

"My name is Abigail, Abigail Andrews, but you can call me Abby." As she reached her hand out to the girl, she noticed a sparkle in her new friend's dark, brown eyes. As the girl started to shake Abby's hand, she hesitated.

"Wait, I've seen that name before. Isn't that the name of this ship?"

"Yes, it is," Abby replied, "it's named after me."

The girl smiled and continued to shake Abby's hand. "My name is Megan Dixon; I'm the captain's daughter."

"You must be on this ship often and know all about it." Abby's voice was filled with wonder.

"Even better," Megan said, "I know a lot about this ocean, and I can tell you anything you want to know." Abby was ready to ask her new friend some questions, but she was drawn to something that glittered in Megan's hair. When Abby looked closer, she saw it was a mermaid hair clip.

"That's a pretty hair clip. Do you like mermaids?" Abby asked, barely holding in her excitement.

"I don't just like them—I love them!" Megan shouted while gently touching her clip. "I have a lot of mermaid artifacts and books in my cabin. Do you want to see them?" Before Abby could answer, she felt Megan's hand grasp hers, and they ran to the bow of the ship, towards a staircase that led to a lower deck. As the two reached the staircase, a little girl walked up the last step with a bucket of soapy water in one hand and a sponge in the other.

Abby watched her old, torn dress drag on the deck as she bent down onto her knees, setting the bucket down beside her. Her hair was wrapped up in an ocean blue scarf that was just as old and torn as her dress. Abby stopped and watched as the girl quietly started to scrub the deck.

"Who's that?" Abby asked Megan.

"Her name is Cora. When she was really young, my dad kept seeing her on the main island. She would always sit on the rocks by herself and stare out into the ocean. One day, he finally went up to talk to her. He learnt that she had no family, and she was always fleeing from her orphanage because she felt a strong connection to the ocean. My dad wanted to help her, so he brought her onto the ship, and she's been here ever since. She likes to help out on board as much as she can to show her appreciation, and she usually wears her tattered clothes when she helps out. When she's not helping out, you can find her on the top deck, watching the ocean," Megan explained.

"What happened to her parents?" Abby asked.

"No one knows," Megan said as she tugged Abby's hand. "Let's go! I can't wait to show you my cabin." Abby continued to follow Megan down the stairs but turned back to look at Cora once more. It was then when something shiny caught Abby's eye; it stood out among the rags like a single rose in a thorn bush. She saw a beautiful locket dangling from Cora's necklace. She wondered why an orphan would have such a nice piece of jewellery and concluded that someone from the ship must have given it to her. Cora looked up and gave Abby a kind smile. Abby smiled back before she turned around to continue heading down the stairs. As much as she wanted to get a closer look at the locket, she wanted to see Megan's cabin more.

When they reached the bottom of the stairs, Abby felt the ship slow down.

"Are we stopping?" She asked.

"Yes, we're stopping at a tiny island so people can leave the ship for the day," Megan said as she stared at Abby with a curious look on her face. "Can you keep a secret? I've had a feeling that I could trust you as soon as I met you. This ship has your name after all."

"I'm very good at keeping secrets. What is it?" Abby was itching to know what Megan wanted to tell her.

"Since we're stopping, I can show you." Megan pulled on Abby's hand and started walking faster, and Abby knew that she must be excited to show her the secret. It was difficult to keep up with every quick step that Megan took. The girls' strides continued to pick up speed until they stopped in front of an engraved wooden door with a giant letter 'M' near the top. Abby knew that they had arrived at Megan's cabin.

Her room wasn't big; it was large enough for a bed, a dresser, and a bookshelf. Abby couldn't believe how many books Megan had. She continued to look around and saw mermaid posters plastered on the walls and different merfolk statues that sat on her dresser. All of the statues looked like they were carved from a pale, grey stone—all except one. Megan ran to that special statue of a realistic, beautiful mermaid who was resting on a rock. She lifted it and dug her fingers in the hollow part underneath, pulling out a key. She then darted to a wall beside her bookshelf and gently pulled a poster off of the wall, exposing a hidden door with a small keyhole.

She turned to Abby and had a huge grin on her face. "Are you ready?" she asked. With a nod of her head, Megan pushed in the key and gently turned it. Abby could feel the anticipation build, and her body started to shake as the door creaked open. Just when she felt like she would burst, the door fully opened, and Abby froze in shock as Megan's secret was revealed.

Chapter Three

Megan's Secret

Though the door led out to the majestic ocean, it was the mystical mermaid in front of the door who had mesmerized Abby.

"Abby, meet my friend Pearl," Megan said proudly. "She is the queen of the merfolk on a secret island not far from here. Pearl, this is Abigail, like the name on the ship." Megan leaned over and put her arm around Abby, gently nudging her forward.

"It's very nice to meet you, Abby. You must be very special as you are the first friend of Megan's that I've met." Pearl said as she smiled. At first, Abby stood still and was enchanted by Pearl's beauty. Her eyes were such a deep sapphire that when Abby looked into them, she felt like she was staring into the ocean. With the sun's rays reflecting down onto her, a halo-like glow surrounded the top of her black, curly hair, and the sun made her silver fins gleam like a million tiny diamonds. She then noticed that Pearl's cropped shirt was the same shade of green as Abby's favourite T-shirt, and she smiled with pride.

Abby stood in admiration for a moment until she broke her silence. "It's nice to meet you, too. I'm sorry for not responding quickly, but I've always wished to meet a mermaid, and I can't believe it's happening. How did you meet Megan?" Just like Abby's adventures in the past, she had so many questions that she didn't know where to start.

"One day, when I was in my cabin, I noticed a tiny beam of light that stretched across my wall. I followed it, and it was coming from behind my bookshelf. I took my books off and slid the shelf over and found the hidden door. The light was coming from the little keyhole. I had stumbled across the key when I first moved into the cabin. I didn't know what it was, so I put it away for safekeeping. As soon as I found the door, I knew what the key was for! I was so curious that I opened the door right away, just in time to see Pearl swimming by. My father keeps telling me that my persistent curiosity would get me in trouble one day, but so far, I've been really lucky!" Megan's face lit up, and Abby could tell that Megan waited a long time to share her secret with someone.

"Why were you near the ship?" Abby asked Pearl.

"There's something about this ship that keeps drawing me in," Pearl explained as she swept a curl off of her face. "I don't know what it is, but I feel like I need to be close to it."

"I think it's because she knew I needed a friend," Megan smiled.

"Since you seem to love merfolk as much as Megan, would you like to meet more of us?" Pearl asked Abby. "I can take you back to our island where you can meet Fin; he's the king and my husband."

Abby couldn't believe what she was hearing. She was so thrilled that she couldn't contain her answer, and it came booming out of her little body. "Yes!"

"Come with me, Abby! We need scuba gear—I have extra gear, and I'll teach you how to put it on and use it!" Megan was so happy that her response came out in a squeal. "Wait here, Pearl, and stay hidden. We'll be right back; we just have to ask for permission."

Once Megan found her father and asked for approval to explore, the girls quickly went to the equipment lockers near the engine room where they grabbed the scuba gear and raced back. Megan showed Abby how to put on the wetsuit, mask, oxygen tank, and fins. After Megan demonstrated how to use everything safely, she double-checked their equipment and confirmed they were ready to go. They joined Pearl in the water, and they were eager to follow her to the secret island.

Before they began swimming, Pearl turned around to make sure the girls were close by. When she turned, Abby noticed something on Pearl's shoulder; she had a cluster of freckles that resembled a seashell.

"What's that, Pearl? Is that a birthmark?" Abby asked, pointing to the freckle cluster. "Well, sort of. It's called the mark of the ocean. All merfolk are born with one," Pearl explained, giving Abby a quick wink before swimming ahead and diving down. Abby followed and dove under the water, but she found it difficult to keep up with Pearl as the beauty of the ocean depths distracted her.

Plants and corals of different shapes, sizes, and colours emerged from the ocean's dark, dull bottom. Abby's favourite coral was bright pink with darker pink spots. It was very tall and its branches reached out, just like the branches of an apple tree. Different plants moved elegantly with the gentle motion of the water; they looked like they were dancing.

A part of Abby felt like staying and dancing with them, but she knew she wanted to meet the merfolk more.

Abby looked up and noticed Megan waving to her, trying to get her attention. When Abby nodded back, Megan began to point, and Abby's eyes followed Megan's finger to a school of more than twenty fish. They were smaller with scales of orange and white. She knew exactly what they were because the tank in her school library had the same ones; these little fish were clownfish. Abby would always peer through the tank glass, making fishy faces at them. She smiled through her mask and waved at the fish as if they understood.

She was entranced by her surroundings, and before she knew it, she was following Pearl and Megan into a dark cave. Her body softly trembled as she continued to swim through the long, narrow tunnel. She was no longer surrounded by the comfort of the ocean's beauty but a colder and sombre environment. Abby slowly stopped shaking as she noticed a small circle of light, but just as she was about to swim towards it, Pearl and Megan made a quick dash to the right. Abby took their lead and she found herself in an even darker tunnel! Though Abby trusted Pearl, she was frightened of the cave's darkness. Butterflies fluttered in her stomach as she lost view of both Pearl and Megan.

Abby quickly started to feel alone in the dark. Her body was still, but her heart raced. She became more frightened as she remembered reading about the dangers that lie in the darkest parts of the ocean. Abby was lost in fear when she felt something grab onto her arm, pulling her upwards through a hole on the top of the cave, leading her to the surface. It happened so fast that Abby couldn't fight it— up she went.

Chapter Four

A New Island

The force pulling Abby stopped after she emerged halfway out of the water. She quickly turned around and was relieved to see Megan and Pearl.

"Sorry for grabbing you like that, Abby." Megan put her arm on Abby's shoulder to comfort her. "I knew you didn't see us, and I couldn't get your attention."

Abby swam forward until her feet could touch the bottom of the ocean floor and she lifted her mask. "That's alright," Abby started to say, but she was distracted by her new surroundings. She was at a small island that was covered in white sand with patches of bright green grass, and in the middle of the grass laid smooth shale rocks. Abby had never seen giant, brown rocks like that before, but all she could focus on were the different merfolk resting on top of each rock. Other merfolk swam and splashed in the crystal-clear waters that surrounded that part of the island. She quickly glanced up to see the clear, blue skies, and a sparkle came to Abby's eye when she saw a huge, double rainbow stretch across the island. As the sun illuminated the scene, it painted a magical picture and Abby felt calm.

"Welcome to Mermaid Tides!" Pearl said as she stretched her arm out and motioned to her little piece of paradise. As kind as it was to have Pearl greet her, it wasn't needed as the warmth and beauty of Mermaid Tides was welcoming all on its own.

As Abby took in the view, a merman swam up to Pearl and hugged her in a loving embrace.

"You must be Fin, the king. I'm Abby," she said as she reached out her hand. The merman released Pearl and stretched out his arm to shake Abby's hand. He was slightly bigger than Pearl and resting on the top of his short wavy blond hair was a small golden crown.

"It's very nice to meet you, Abby. We hardly have visitors to our island, so this is a real treat." Fin gently let go of Abby's hand, and she noticed that his eyes were the colour of the grass that surrounded the island. He then turned and nodded to Megan with a smile. "Megan, it's nice to see you again."

"It's nice to see you too," Megan said with a shy giggle.

"This is such a beautiful place; how come it's a secret?" Abby asked and watched as Pearl and Fin exchanged worried looks.

"We're afraid that's a long story, Abby. You must understand that not all people are as trusting and as nice as you," Fin explained, "some people have bad intentions and can't keep our secret. They're eager to tell the world that we exist, and they do it at a price. Some try to find our unique artifacts to sell or keep."

"Oh no!" Abby exclaimed. "Have people already made attempts?" Abby's question was met by a brief silence. The mood quickly changed to that of fear as Abby waited for her answer.

"Some come and go, but one man has always made attempts to not only find and steal our possessions, but he has tried to take us as well. He's known to collect and scavenge rare items and attempts to sell them for a lot of money. He scours the ocean for anything found in urban legends; unique treasures and any item not yet seen by mankind. About seven years ago, one of our mermaids accidentally let herself be seen by this man while she was out for a long swim. Since then, he's made many attempts to steal our things and kidnap us. To him, we're the rarest item he could have in his possession. We call him the Scavenger, and we fear he won't stop until he gets what he wants."

"Has he ever succeeded in getting anything?" Abby asked quietly, feeling terrible that someone could cause this much fear. She looked at the king and the queen as silence filled the air once again. Pearl glanced at Fin with sad eyes.

"Yes. Because of the Scavenger, we lost one of our most precious gifts," Fin answered as he put an arm around Pearl.

"Was it rare and expensive?" Abby asked.

"Yes, it was very rare and priceless." He answered as Pearl began to swim away from the group. Abby was very curious about the item the Scavenger had taken from them. From Pearl's reaction, Abby could tell it was really important to them. She wanted to ask more questions, but her thoughts were interrupted by a loud noise that sounded like a boat motor, followed by many screams.

"He's here, hide!" One mermaid shouted before disappearing into the water. All the other merfolk scattered in fear.

"It's the Scavenger, he must have followed you!" Fin shouted as he searched for his wife in a panic. Abby couldn't see much in the chaos, but she could tell that there was a small ship with what looked like a giant robotic arm coming out of it. The ship was moving towards them, extending its arm closer, and something was in its grip. It was hard to see what it was, but it was big enough to cast a shadow over them. As the shadow grew larger, Abby could tell that it was right over them. A hush fell over the island and all Abby could hear was her heart beating in fear.

The silence was quickly broken as the arm released the giant object above them. The next sound she heard was the booming voice of Fin, "Dive down!"

Chapter Five

The Pursuit

As the darkness cleared, so did some of Abby's fear, and after all of the chaos, she and her new friends remained silent. She slowly poked her head out of the water and noticed that the ship was gone, and the merfolk cautiously started to emerge from their hiding spots.

"Is everyone ok?" Fin asked once he surfaced.

"I think so," Abby replied. She was still trying to understand what had happened. She glanced over at Megan, who gave Abby a reassuring nod. "If the Scavenger is gone, does that mean he got what he came for?"

"Oh no, Pearl!" Fin shouted as he swam over to where he last saw his wife. "She's gone."

"He took Pearl?" Abby asked, realizing that it must have been a large net that dropped. "We must find her before he uses her to expose the merfolk!" Abby was ready to search for Pearl until she realized she didn't know where she was heading. "Do you know where the Scavenger would've taken her?"

"He has a lair close by. I don't know where it is, but I can use Pearl to find it," said Fin in a hopeful tone.

"I don't understand. Pearl isn't here to help." Abby tilted her head in confusion.

"Abby, all the merfolk can sense each other," Megan replied. "Pearl told me when we first met. It's like a sixth sense that makes their heart tingle and their body fill with warmth when they get close to one another."

"Megan's right, but you girls must stay here. It's too dangerous for you to come with me," Fin stated.

"There's no way that's happening!" Abby exclaimed as she lowered her facemask. Abby knew there was a reason she ended up on that ship; she needed to help Fin and Pearl.

"Abby's right, Pearl's our friend, and we want to save her as much as you do. I'm used to the water; I can help guide." Megan said as she lowered her facemask as well.

The king knew that he wouldn't be able to win this battle without the girls, so he reluctantly agreed. He also knew that the Scavenger would not expect them, so it gave them a secret advantage. "Well then, I hope you girls are ready," he said as he swam in front of them. "I can sense her over here," Fin said, pointing his finger north, "let's go!" He quickly dove down, and the girls followed.

They started at the tunnel where Abby once felt lost and scared, but this time, she was comforted by her confidence. She followed Megan and Fin out of the cave, and they circled the same school of clownfish. Abby smiled and waved once again to the beautiful fish. She giggled to herself when she thought about how a group of fish was called a school, and she thought of how funny it would be if they had a playground and fought over the swings too. Abby shook her head, trying to focus on the task at hand as the three moved in a different direction. Even though she knew they were on an important mission, she was excited to see new parts of the ocean.

She was so amazed by all the sights that she didn't notice Megan and Fin had stopped swimming. She tried to stop but ended up softly bumping into Megan. Megan didn't turn around, though; she gently held her arm back, indicating that Abby shouldn't move. Abby then looked over to Fin, who was just as still. Both of his arms were out as if he was trying to protect the girls. Abby didn't understand what was going on, so without creating a lot of movement, she tried to look around. Her eyes finally caught a glimpse of the problem: heading straight for them was a tiger shark.

Chapter Six

Ocean's Pearl

Terror filled Abby's soul as the giant, striped, grey shark slowly swam towards them. Her fear worsened when she saw teeth peek out of its mouth. The three stayed motionless in hopes that the shark would see there was no need to harm them. Abby felt like the shark could see her chest move as her heart pounded, making her more nervous. She wanted to close her eyes in fear, but she kept them open in case she needed to act quickly.

Just as the shark got closer, it turned very slightly, and Abby realized it was just passing by. It was so close to her that she could feel its cool skin brush against her leg. With every inch the shark moved by her, Abby's nerves grew, and it took everything she had to stop her body from quivering.

Once the shark passed them and continued to swim in the opposite direction, the three friends slowly turned their heads to ensure the shark was clearly out-of-sight. A feeling of relief washed over them, and their shoulders dropped as the tension left their bodies. Fin turned to the girls to make sure they were okay to keep moving. Both Abby and Megan gave him a thumbs up and off they went.

They swam further and noticed the water getting shallow as they reached a large cave that was half emerged in the water and half out. They swam just on top of the surface and went through the entrance; Abby knew she was in the right place when she recognized the

Scavenger's ship that was anchored to the far
right.

They thought the Scavenger would be waiting
for them, so they dove down to find another
way in. Abby instantly saw an opening on the
cave wall and knew it had to be a tunnel. Fin
saw it too and rushed over, motioning for the
girls to follow. As they made their way through
the narrow passageway, Abby saw different
openings that led in different directions. It was
as if they were in a maze under the cave!
Darkness grew the further they went in and
before the girls realized they had lost sight of
Fin.

Abby looked at Megan with hope that her
scuba skills and ocean instincts would lead
them in the right direction. Megan gave Abby a
quick thumbs-up before taking charge, and she
led Abby through the maze. Abby was worried
about how long they were in there, but she saw

a light and knew they had reached the surface. The girls slowly swam up and poked their heads out of the water, just enough to peek out.

They found themselves in a small crevice in the cave floor with brown rock walls surrounding them. The walls had different impressions that acted like shelves for the many artifacts the Scavenger had stored. Green vines stood out against the dull rock and softly looped around the artifacts as if they were protecting them. Abby had trouble identifying the items among the vines and dust, but she spotted an antique jewellery box with a bright red ruby on the front.

Before Abby could study more of the items, she heard a man's voice and knew it was the Scavenger. Both girls followed the sound of the voice and they stopped swimming when they saw a short, stout man with white hair. His hair was very thin, but the small amount he had was spiked in the front. He had a large, slightly crooked nose that held a thick pair of black glasses. Abby was delighted when she looked past the scary man and saw Pearl. She wasn't harmed, but she was in a crevice of water that was surrounded by a metal gate. She was trapped.

"I know you can do it; sing your magical song and this will all be over!" The Scavenger angrily shouted at Pearl.

"I don't know what you're talking about, and I won't sing a word!" Pearl shouted back. "If you could just explain what you want, maybe I can help you find it."

"I'm looking for the Ocean's Pearl, as one of my books referred to. It's known to turn humans into merfolk and merfolk into humans. There was no description; it just had a passage that said *it holds all the power in a song to take you where you truly belong.* You're the queen of this ocean, and your name is Pearl, so you have to be what I'm looking for. You know what you need to do, so get on with it!" The Scavenger demanded as he clenched his fist, raising it in the air with frustration.

The girls lifted their heads a little higher and Megan quickly turned to Abby. "I don't think Pearl is what he's looking for. She told me that the only power she has is to sense other merfolk. I don't think she'd lie to me. She told me that she trusted me," Megan whispered. "There has to be something else."

"You're probably right. If we find the real Ocean's Pearl, we can try to trade it for Pearl."

"I bet we could find something in one of my books back on the ship." The sparkle returned to Megan's eyes as she realized her books could help save Pearl.

"You're right, we should go, but we should try to find Fin first." Abby was curious to where Fin was, but she realized that he must have taken another tunnel.

The girls were getting ready to leave when Fin rose from the water, causing waves to splash loudly against the cave wall. Before they could react, a shadow overtook the light. Abby shuddered as she knew the shadow belonged to the Scavenger and that he was standing right over them.

Chapter Seven

An Orphan's Secret

Fin shoved the girls out of the way and the Scavenger grabbed him. Knowing that they could save him and Pearl if they found what the Scavenger was looking for, Megan and Abby went under the water and quickly swam away. Once they reached the surface and met up with Megan's father's docked cruise ship, Megan frantically rubbed her hands along the side of the ship, feeling for the secret door. Her hands stopped and she pushed forward. The door slowly opened, and Megan pulled herself into her cabin and helped Abby on board before darting over to her bookshelf.

"Oh no!" Megan proclaimed, "I left the book that I need on the top deck!" She ran out of her cabin and up the stairs, stripping off her scuba gear at the same time.

"Behind you!" Abby shouted back as she ran behind Megan while also removing her scuba gear. By the time the girls reached the top of the stairs, they were in their wetsuits. Abby raced on the deck, trying to keep up, but she wasn't watching where she was going.

Bang! Abby crashed into someone and fell to the ground. She gave her head a shake and saw Cora on the floor beside her.

"I'm so sorry, Cora," Abby said as she dusted herself off and got up. "Let me help you up." Abby bent down and offered her hand to Cora.

"That's okay, I wasn't watching where I was going," Cora said as she accepted Abby's hand and got back up. "Should I know you?" Cora asked in confusion.

"This is Abby. She's a friend of mine and I told her your name," Megan replied. She had heard the crash and came back to make sure Abby and Cora were alright.

"It's nice to officially meet you," Abby said. She was about to shake Cora's hand when something shiny on the ground caught her eye. Right away, Abby knew it was the locket she noticed earlier that day. It must have fallen off Cora when they collided. This time, it looked a little different; it had opened, and light was bouncing off something inside of it. The mysterious object was a glistening white colour and looked familiar to Abby. "Is this a pearl?" Abby asked as she picked up the locket.

"Yes, I think it is," Cora replied.

"Where did you get this? How long have you had it?" Questions started to flow out of

Abby. She had a feeling that the locket was more than just a necklace.

"I've had it as long as I could remember. I was told that it was found with me, along with a note from my mother."

"Do you know what the note said?" Abby asked.

"Yes, but I never understood it. All it said was *this holds all the power in a song to take you where you truly belong.*"

"The Ocean's Pearl! Abby we found it!" Megan shouted in excitement as she snatched the locket out of Abby's hands and went back down the stairs.

"Megan, wait!" Abby ran after her with Cora following. The girls followed Megan back to her cabin.

"That's mine, Megan. Please give it back," Cora said sadly, reaching out her open hand.

"Sorry, Cora, I don't want to upset you, but you don't understand," Megan said. Megan began filling Cora in on the day's events and as she did, Cora's tattered sleeve slid off of her shoulder. As she went to adjust it, Abby caught a glimpse of a group of freckles that looked just like a seashell.

"The mark of the ocean . . . you have it." Abby pointed to Cora's shoulder.

"What do you mean? It's just a birthmark," Cora said as she pulled her sleeve back up. Even though Megan was excited about the mark, she held it together and finished telling Cora about their day, including the merfolk and the mark of the ocean.

"I can't believe what I'm hearing!" Cora was so shocked that she wasn't sure if she understood everything.

"May I see that?" Abby reached for the locket. After Megan handed it to her, she studied it carefully and noticed words engraved on the inside, opposite of the pearl. "Have you read this out loud before?" Abby asked Cora.

"I can't read; no one has ever taught me." Cora lowered her head in sadness. Abby put her hand on Cora's shoulder to comfort her and she began to read the inscription out loud.

"Sing your special song. Sing it more and more. I want to find what I've been longing for." Once Abby finished reading, music poured out of the locket and filled the air. It was a sweet tune that sounded like a lullaby. As the music got louder, a strong gust of wind blew the ocean blue scarf off of Cora's head revealing long, black curls. The wind was so strong that Abby closed her eyes for just a second. When she opened them again, she instantly noticed that Cora was different. She was now a beautiful mermaid. Abby turned to Megan to see her reaction to Cora's transformation, but Megan wasn't looking at Cora, she was looking at Abby in shock. That's when Abby realized Cora wasn't the only one who had changed.

Chapter Eight

Who Needs Legs?

Abby looked down at where her legs once were and instead, she saw sparkling blue scales, the same colour of her favourite overalls. She couldn't believe it—she was a mermaid! She pushed herself through the secret door and into the water before turning around to help Cora into the water with her.

"That's not fair, how come I didn't change?" Megan asked, crossing her arms.

"The locket's song is supposed to take us where we belong, so Cora and I must need to be mermaids right now. It must be the same for you; you must need to be human. We can find out why this happened once we go back to the lair to save Fin and Pearl!"

"You're right, Abby," Megan said and uncrossed her arms, "You two go ahead, I'll get my scuba gear back on and I'll be close behind you."

"It's probably safer if we all stick together," Abby suggested.

"It's okay, I'll be careful, and I won't be too far behind. You need to go!" Megan insisted, running to the stairs to collect all of her gear.

"She's right. Hurry, Cora, we need to go fast! I remember where it is; you can follow me." Abby put the locket around her neck for safekeeping since she knew the Scavenger was really after it and she wanted to keep Cora safe. Abby grabbed Cora's hand and led her under the water. It didn't take the girls long to figure out how to use their fins and fast. Abby was having so much fun, and she felt so free that she had to keep reminding herself of her mission and that it wasn't time to play. It was hard, but luckily their destination was in sight.

When the girls found their way to the Scavenger's lair, Abby dove down and led Cora through the maze of tunnels.

While Abby was figuring out which way to go, Cora grabbed her hand and stopped her from going forward. Abby turned around and watched as Cora placed her hand over her heart. Abby knew what was going on; Cora was sensing Fin and Pearl. As a new mermaid, Abby thought it would be an overwhelming feeling for her. She couldn't feel them, but she knew that she didn't have the ocean's mark and she wasn't truly a mermaid. Abby nodded to Cora, showing her that it was okay.

The girls slowly continued until thcy reached a dead end, but as Abby examined the wall, she saw a light peek through a tiny crack on the side. A feeling of hope poured over her as she realized it was a door! She pointed it out to Cora, and the girls started searching for a way to open it. Cora swam a few feet away and returned with a stick. She wedged it in between the crack, and she and Abby pushed it away from them. Since they were working together, it didn't take much time to open the door.

Abby swam through the door first to make sure they weren't heading straight for a trap. She put her hand down to stop Cora, indicating that she needed to stay there. Cora understood and stayed behind the entrance. Abby continued on and saw shadows in the water as she got closer—she knew it was Pearl and Fin. She was really excited knowing that she and Cora had just found a way to get them out of their water prison. Abby was going to signal for Cora to come and join her, but she decided that she had a smaller chance of being noticed if it was just her, so she continued without her.

Abby peered through the water towards the surface. She couldn't see the Scavenger nearby, so she decided that it was safe to go up. She slowly swam up beside the king and queen to get their attention. Abby noticed that Pearl's hand was floating by her side, and when she reached out to grab it, a shadow appeared over her. Before she could react, someone grabbed Abby's arm and pulled her out of the water.

Chapter Nine

A Gift Returned

The Scavenger pulled Abby through an open part of the metal gate, which closed as soon as she was out.

"You're one of the girls who got away, and now you're a mermaid. That means you found the Ocean's Pearl!" he exclaimed. Before he could ask where it was, he noticed Abby's locket. "What do we have here?" He reached out for it, but Abby started to wiggle, making it difficult for him to grab it. As she continued to twist and turn, she saw Megan out of the corner of her eye, sneaking behind the Scavenger and towards the metal gate. Abby was relieved to see she had made it to the lair and had used the same tunnel as before. Abby wiggled even more to distract the Scavenger from what was happening behind him.

Megan searched for the rope that would lift the gate to free Fin and Pearl. She didn't know that Abby and Cora had discovered another way out, but it took her no time at all to find the rope, just a few feet from the gate. As Megan reached for it, the Scavenger was finally able to get his hands around the locket, but he was startled when the gate quickly rose. The commotion made him release Abby and the locket. Abby knew that she needed to act quickly, so she spun around and pushed him into the water. *Splash!* He waved his arms about, trying to climb back on the crevice ledge. Just as he was about to pull himself back up, Fin surprised the Scavenger from behind and grabbed him. He tried to wiggle himself free, but Fin's grip was too powerful.

"Please, I need that locket!" the Scavenger cried out.

"No, you're just going to sell it for money and expose the merfolk!" Abby stated as she turned and dipped her fins into the water to keep her scales wet. "Their secret must not be revealed as it will put them all in danger."

"You don't understand! That's not why I want it, I promise," he replied.

"Let's hear him out," Pearl said, swimming in front of him.

"For my entire life, I felt like I didn't belong. I never made friends as a young boy, and I always knew that I didn't fit in with the other children. I spent a lot of time alone, so I'd always go to the library and read books about the ocean. With every word I read and every picture I saw, this feeling inside of me grew.

It's as if the ocean was calling me. That's where I want to be."

"You want to become a merman?" Abby asked in disbelief.

"Yes, that's all I've ever wanted," he said with a sad voice. "I studied the legends of the merfolk and wished so hard that it was true. I'd close my eyes at night and become a merman in my dreams. It was at night when I was alive and free. A part of me thought that I would never be that merman. I tried to do the next best thing: spend time in the ocean, collecting things that kept me close to it. When I caught a glimpse of your friend in the water many years ago, my hope was restored." He shrugged his shoulders and lowered his head in defeat. "I'm sorry for all the bad things I've done and the problems that I've caused. I was trying to chase you because I was trying to chase my dreams."

Abby got an idea, and a huge smile came to her face. "If he's really meant to be a merman, then the song of the Ocean's Pearl will turn him into one." Abby opened up the locket and was ready to read the inscription.

"You're right, Abby. Let's give it a try." Fin gave Abby the permission she was waiting for, so Abby read the words out loud and a familiar song filled the air. As expected, the wind rose quickly, but this time it was so powerful that water splashed over the Scavenger and throughout the cave.

As it splashed over Abby, she closed her eyes like she did before, but this time she knew what she would see when she opened them. Just as she thought, the Scavenger was now a merman.

His hair was thicker, and he removed his glasses because he could see without them. He was so happy, it was clear he was telling the truth; he truly belonged in the ocean. He gave Abby a smile before swimming down towards the tunnel to explore his new world.

Abby was happy to see him in his rightful place, but she was even happier to see that her legs returned. Even though she loved the freedom she felt while she was a mermaid, she knew it wasn't where she belonged.

"Abby, did you forget about me?" A little voice came from behind Pearl and Fin, causing them to turn around quickly.

"Oh, sorry!" Abby started to apologize to Cora, who had missed a lot of the commotion as she had stayed right where Abby had left her. "Pearl, Fin, this is . . ."

"Coral, it can't be!" Pearl cried out before Abby finished her introduction. Pearl swam over and gave Cora a loving embrace.

"How do you know my full name?" Cora asked as Pearl let her go.

"You're our daughter," Fin said as he took a turn to sweep Cora into his arms. "Abby, where did you find her?"

"She was on the ship the whole time, but as a human!" Megan answered as she didn't want to be left out of the conversation.

"That's why I was always drawn to that ship; a part of me could sense you," Pearl said in amazement. "Since you weren't in mermaid form, the feeling wasn't strong enough for me to know it was you."

"How come you gave me up?" Cora asked as a tear rolled down her face. Pearl softly wiped the tear away and held her little girl in her arms.

"We didn't want to, Cora," Fin started to explain. "When we first learned about the Scavenger and how he came to Mermaid Tides, we thought you were in danger. We used the locket to change you into a human, and we dropped you off on the shoreline beside an orphanage. We waited close by to make sure someone from the orphanage found you. It was the hardest thing we've ever had to do, but it was our only guarantee that you would be safe. Rumours built the Scavenger up to be a very dangerous man. Your mom sent the note and the locket with you, knowing that one day you'd find your way back to us. It was lucky that you had it because just days after we hid you, the Scavenger came back and took the ruby jewellery box that held the locket."

As Abby watched Fin wrap his arms around his wife and daughter, her heart was filled with joy. In that moment, Abby realized that the priceless and precious gift they lost years ago was Cora.

As she continued to watch the touching reunion, a thought came to Abby. She rushed over to one of the cave walls and grabbed the antique jewellery box she had spotted earlier.

"I think this belongs to you," Abby said as she wiped the dust away before handing the box to Pearl.

"That's it! Now we can keep the locket where it belongs," Pearl said as she turned towards Abby and Megan. "Girls, we can't thank you enough for all that you've done for us. Both of you will forever be honorary mermaids and part of our family."

"I'm glad I was a part of it because it was an adventure that I'll never forget," Abby started saying, but before she could continue, she felt a splash of water against her back. When she turned around to see who had splashed her, she felt a warm breeze rustle through her pigtails and she heard magical chimes swirl around her.

"I got you!" Abby's mother laughed as she knelt by the pool. "You must have been having a good time with that toy ship because you didn't notice that I snuck up to splash you."

Abby picked up her favourite pool toy and softly smiled because she knew her day wouldn't have been as much fun without the ship her grandfather had made for her. "What can I say, Mom. It was another amazing adventure."

Ready for More Adventures?

Visit the Abigail Andrews' website to learn more about all of the volumes of, *The Amazing Adventures of Abigail Andrews!*

① Pirate's Playground

② Dr. Swan's Magic Kingdom

③ Pool of Secrets

④ Planetarium Panic

www.AbigailAndrewsSeries.com

About the Author

Nicole Brook, known as Nickie by her friends and family, was raised on a farm near Warburg, Alberta. Hailing from a small-town community, Nicole had big writing aspirations from a young age. She dreamt about being an author and wrote her first novel in the third grade. Just like her main character, Nicole was a blonde-haired, blue-eyed little girl with a wild imagination.

Nicole's fondest childhood memories took place at her great-grandmother's house. Nicole, her brother Curtis, and cousins Jamie and Ashley explored their great-grandmother's farm and played outside for hours.

A new adventure awaited them every time they got together, and they couldn't wait to tell their great-grandmother about their wild excursions. These adventures not only touched her heart but inspired Nicole to write the *Abigail* series.

Currently residing in Leduc, Alberta, Nicole and her husband, Brandon, welcomed their first child, a beautiful girl named Piper, in August of 2013. Nicole had some very memorable moments after the release of her series. She had incredible opportunities to meet a lot of her biggest fans as she toured different bookstores and over seventy-five schools.

In May of 2016, Nicole and Brandon's family grew again, and they welcomed their first son, Axel. Nicole is inspired every day by watching Piper and Axel continue her childhood adventures. She can't wait to meet, teach, and inspire more kids as her journey continues.

Manufactured by Amazon.ca
Bolton, ON